NOTHING BUT WORDS

nkh.i

Haters are going to hate,
Potatoes are going to potate.

nkh.i

Life Pro-tips #1

Most of the time they lie when they say
they are going to stay.

nkh.i

be kind.

we are all only human after all.
nkh.i

your tough times bring out
the worst of people but the best of you.
nkh.i

she was never excellent and never will be.
but all along she has always been herself,
that many did not get to be.
nkh.i

love all with all the love,
but love yourself the most.
nkh.i

just like how you still feel sadness
as if it was yesterday,
even after years, that is how short life is.
nkh.i

to have money is nice.
to have peace of mind is nicer.
to have both is heavenly.

nkh.i

faith of a child, innocent and kind.
pain of a man, wounding and cruel.
oh, so so fragile.
that is all we are.

nkh.i

it is perfectly okay to be yourself.
look at yourself. awesome af.

nkh.i

breathe, baby. breathe.
<hr>
nkh.i

in a world so fast,
take time to slow down and unwind.
nkh.i

at the end of the day,
it is you alone with you.
so feed you, first.
love you, first.

nkh.i

pray for the situations to be easier,
but also pray for you to be stronger.
nkh.i

embrace your ups and downs.
be kindest and softest with yourself.
you need you.

nkh.i

I have my coffee unsweetened
because I know I am the sugar.

nkh.i

hehe.
nkh.i

always love like never before.
so when it is gone,
it will always be their lost.
nkh.i

passion needs patience.
nkh.i

sometimes when I'm sad,
I draw a little, doodle a little.
only to feel my inner child smiling.

nkh.i

abundance, abundance, abundance.
I am blessed.
I am blessed.
I am blessed.
blessing is me.
nkh.i

to do list
   1. live

nkh.i

if you find things funny, laugh.
if you find things sad, cry.
it is okay to show how you feel.
nkh.i

sometimes,
god really sees me as one of
his strongest soldiers.
and I really don't know
how to feel about it.
nkh.i

to disappear away is nice.
but to be found is nicer.

nkh.i

my mother once said,

"make yourself useful in every situation,
but know when they are just using you."

I didn't understand then, now I know.
nkh.i

they can say anything all they want.

your destiny is in your hands,
in your every thoughts and your feelings.
nkh.i

use your energy to create, grow and heal
protect it with your life.

nkh.i

one step at a time.
don't underestimate your little progress.
progress is progress.
nkh.i

it will never be easy
but never invalidate your own feelings.
colors don't change.
a red flag is a red flag.

nkh.i

forgive those who hurt you.
forgive yourself too.

nkh.i

magic. we are all magic.
nobody knows
what is going on on the inside,
but still we make things happen.
magic. we are all magic.

nkh.i

they say never to tell your sadness.
no one cares anyways.
but here I am, writing it all away.
I don't care either.
nkh.i